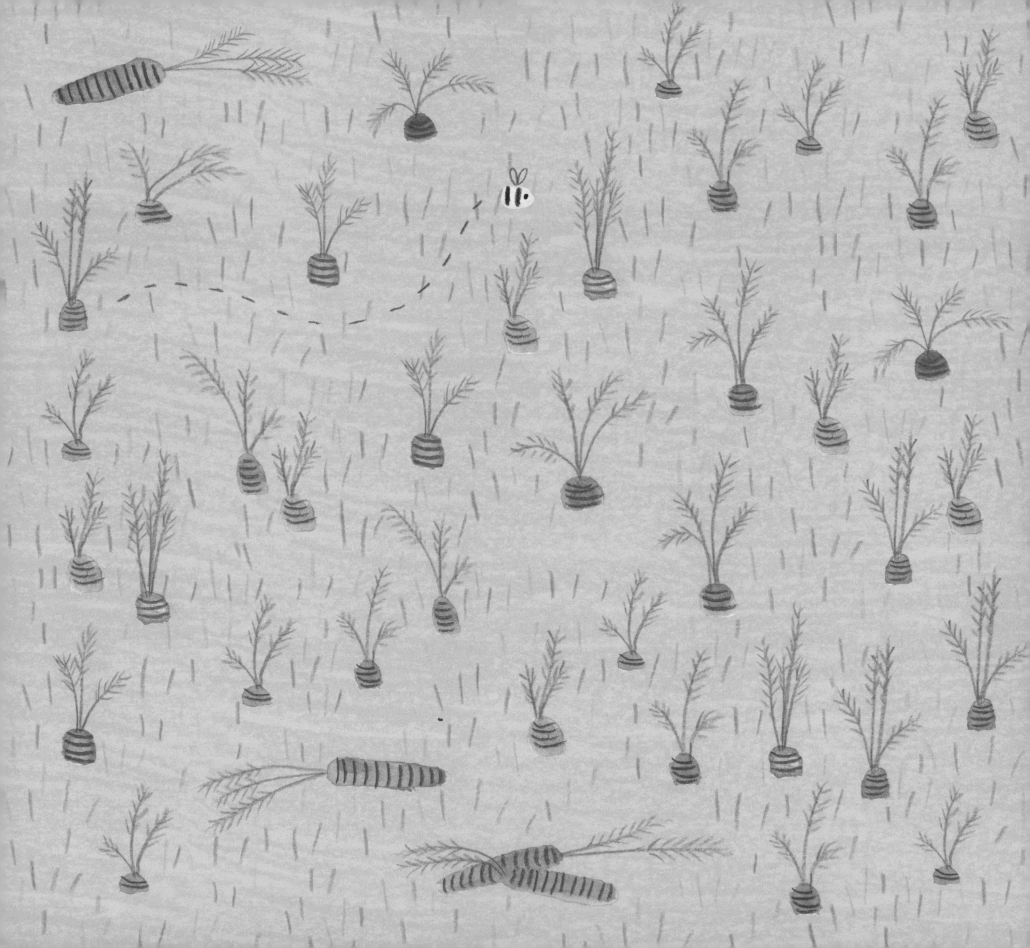

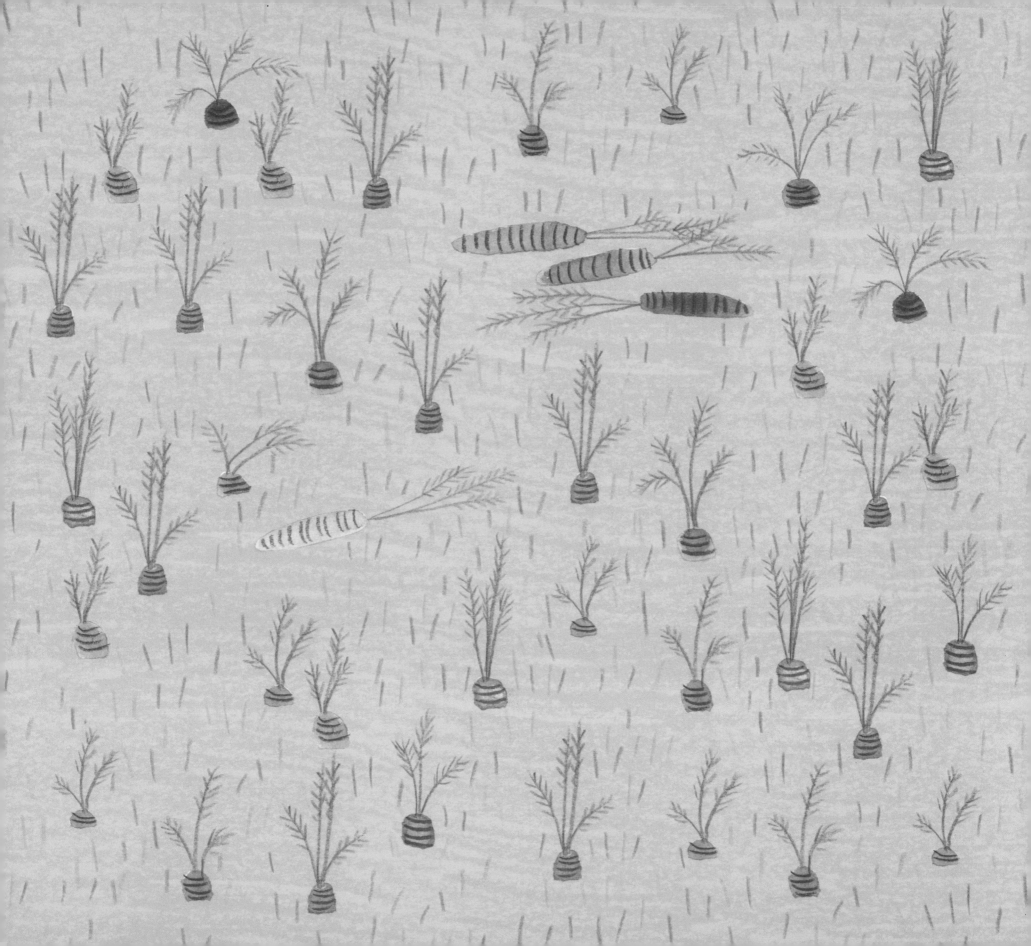

For (begrudgingly) Maisie, Georgia, Felix,
Catherine, Casper, Alice, Kara, Jack and Luke.
I did like being an only child but: the more, the merrier.
– L.S.

First published in 2020 by Scholastic Children's Books
Euston House, 24 Eversholt Street, London NW1 1DB
a division of Scholastic Ltd

www.scholastic.co.uk
London • New York • Toronto • Sydney • Auckland • Mexico City
New Delhi • Hong Kong

Text and illustrations copyright © 2020 Lorna Scobie

ISBN PB 978 1407 19249 9

Printed in China

10 9 8 7 6 5 4 3 2 1

The moral rights of Lorna Scobie have been asserted.

Papers used by Scholastic Children's Books are made from wood
grown in sustainable forests.

No rabbits were harmed in the making of this book.

SCHOLASTIC

FSC
MIX
Paper from
responsible sources
www.fsc.org FSC® C008047

Rabbit! Rabbit! Rabbit!

LORNA SCOBIE

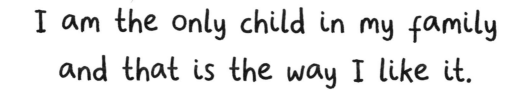

I am the only child in my family
and that is the way I like it.

The fox next door says she likes having rabbits around.

The more, the merrier, she says.

But I can't see why.

My
stretching
area

My bedroom

But my parents have some news.

Suddenly, I am no longer an only child.

Napping in my stretching area →

In my bedroom!

I have to establish some rules.

This works well.

Until . . . .

...my parents have more news.

And more.

And MORE.

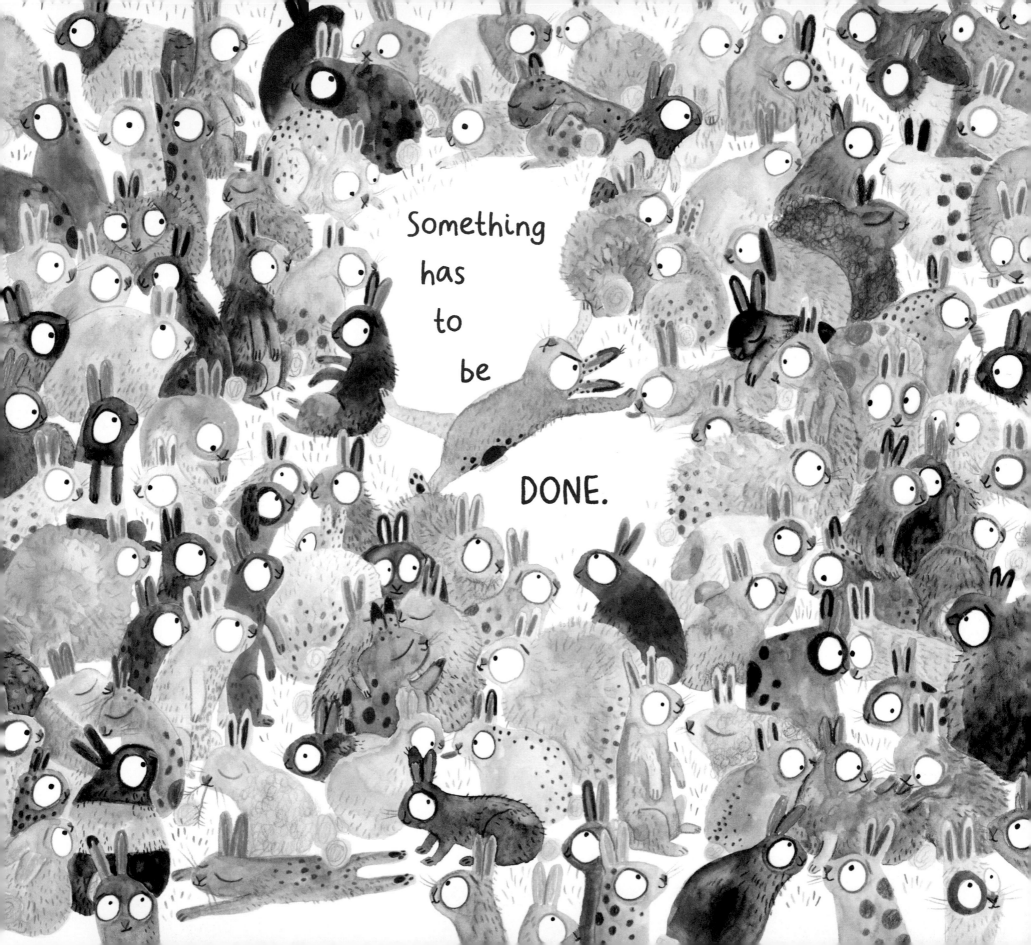

Something
has
to
be

DONE.

I go next door.

Would you like to
come in too?
The more,
the merrier.

OK then, I guess.

And much to my horror . . .

It is quite nice.

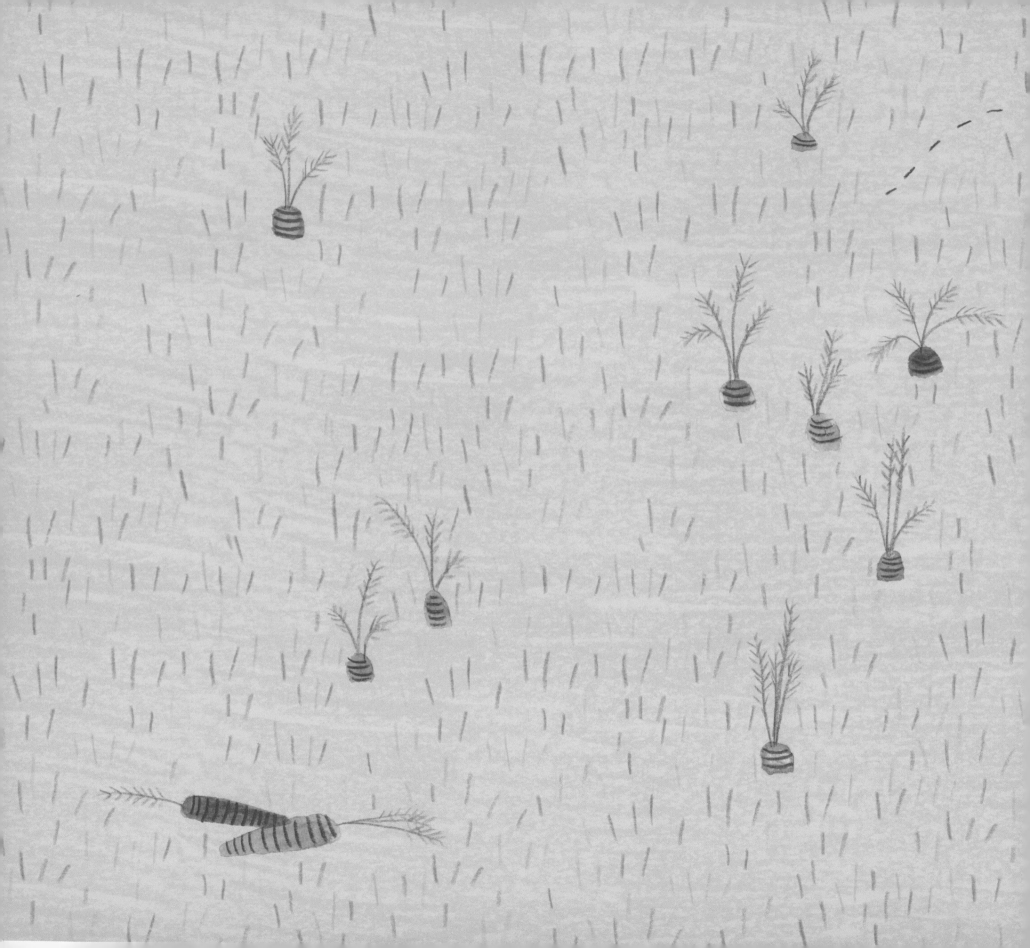

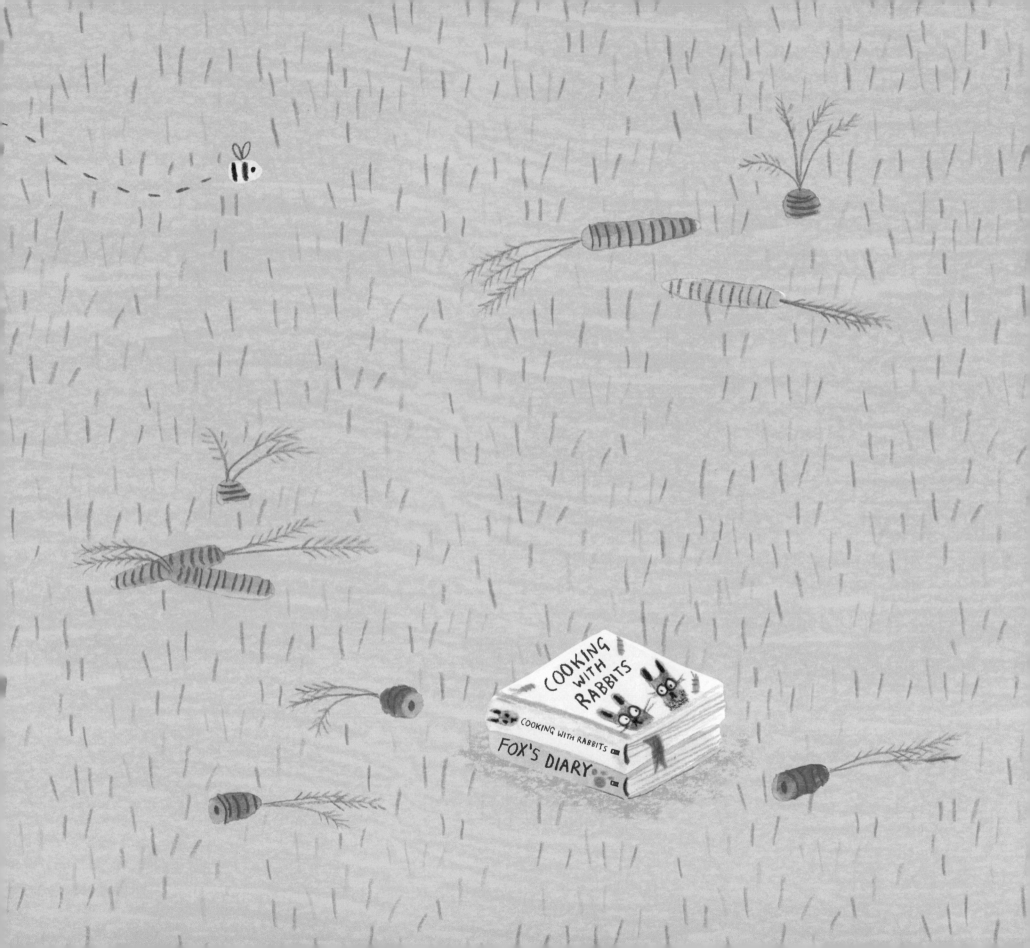